Herr Cherrytree

Idyls Crude

Herr Cherrytree

Idyls Crude

ISBN/EAN: 9783337319342

Printed in Europe, USA, Canada, Australia, Japan

Cover: Foto ©Andreas Hilbeck / pixelio.de

More available books at **www.hansebooks.com**

IDYLS CRUDE.

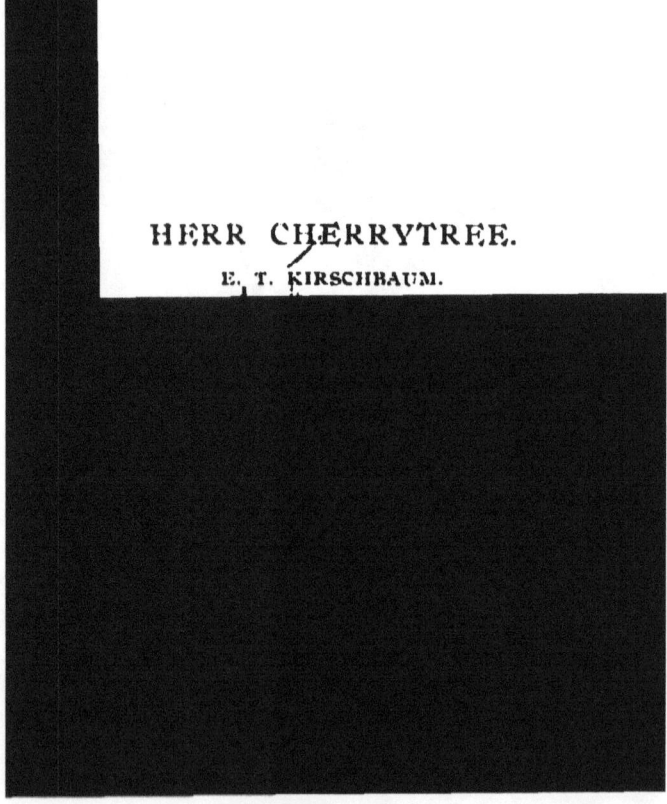

HERR CHERRYTREE.

E. T. KIRSCHBAUM.

WORCESTER.

O. B. WOOD, PUBLISHER

1894.

CONTENTS.

	PAGE
THE SONG OF OCEAN,	7
THY IMAGE LIVES FOREVER,	8
ON THE ACUSHNET,	9
A MYTH,	10
LOVE IS BUT A SLENDER TETHER,	12
TO ONLY SEE WHAT NOW I DREAM,	13
AT NEWPORT CLIFFS,	14
A TALE OF LOVE,	15
THE ESCAPE,	16
THE PUBLIC GIVER,	18
THE BRIDE OF A YEAR,	20
TO A TEAPOT,	22
THE DYING GULL,	23
THE CURSE OF THE DAY,	24
ARE WE PULLING OTHERS DOWN?	26
THE SONG OF THE RIVULET,	28
THEODORE BEANE,	30
BARON MONOPOLY,	31
STILL THE RIVER GLIDES AWAY,	33
DR. G. FELIX MATTHES,	34
THY SONG'S ITS OWN AND GOD WITHIN,	36
ONLY A BRAKEMAN,	37
A LIKELIHOOD,	39
ODE TO A MOSQUITO,	40
DYING ALONE,	42
A CHARACTERISTIC,	44
THE BROKEN VASE,	46
I SAUNTER BY THE COMING TIDE,	48
EIN ZWEITER HANS SACHS (a second Hans Sachs),	49
I WANDERED WITH THE MUSE, APACE,	51
THE MILL ON THE DAMN-SIDE,	52

	PAGE
For a Soldier is in the Room,	54
A Memorial Tribute,	56
Other Days,	57
Life, ...	59
A Poet's Fancy Takes Me,	60
When Some Men Die, . . .	61
Chimes sweet with Music to my Ear,	63
The Poet's Fate, .	64
My Mother's Grave, .	66
Ships that never Sail,	68
Welcome, ...	70
These Words are but its Knell,	72
Peg! Peg! Peg!	73
Time's a Mirror held Before Thee,	75
Discontentment is the Story,	77
The Old Mill at Nantucket,	78
My Song has taken Flight,	80

IDYLS CRUDE.

THE SONG OF OCEAN.

I STROLLED along the ocean's side
Alone in my emotion;
I heard the music of the tide ---
Then came this song of ocean.

"Dost see my waters come and go?
The same will be forever;
From o'er the billows I will flow
Forever and forever."

Eternal, then, this restless glide,
Perpetual its motion!
My life but imitates the tide
Humanity the ocean!

THY IMAGE LIVES FOREVER.

THROUGH my window brightly beaming
Comes the ever silent moon,
    Bringing rapture to my dreaming,
Lighting up my humble room.

Now it falls in silvery splendor
On a worn and empty chair ;
    Calling memories ever tender
Of the one so hard to spare.

Is she sitting now beside me
As I gaze into the light ?   ·
    Is the seeming but a memory
In this mirror of the night?

Aye, though life and death may sever,
Though the grave be thine to-night !
    Yet thy image lives forever
In its own resplendent light !

ON THE ACUSHNET.

—

FAR and wide the flowing river
Glides along its radiant way,
  While the clouds in crimson quiver
Sail away with touch of day.
  All along the bridge and meadows,
Streams the sun in quick'ning glance,
  While at distant panes and windows
Golden sunbeams gaily dance.

At my feet the rippling river
Sweeps along 'mid azure hue,
  While to me the great forever
Bears me seaward in the view;—
  And far out beyond retreating,
Borne along and driven wide
  With the river I'm repeating
Life's reflective greater tide.

A MYTH.

— —

I KNEW her when she came to-day,
  A maiden now full dearer grown —
She came and led me far away
  Through years that she and I had known.

I looked into her own dear eyes,
  They bore the same expression still —
I felt the truth that love implies,
  And gave my heart up to her will.

Her fancy took me to the place
  Where once familiar faces shone —
But all had changed, not e'en a trace
  Of those that we had kindly known.

We sat beneath the cool pine boughs,
  Where evenings of the long ago
We spoke of love, and made the vows
  That only fate could overthrow.

We lingered by the quiet church,
  And peered in through the vestry door —

But fruitless seemed our every search
  To meet some smiling face of yore.

At last we reached the churchyard gate,
  And here I found myself alone —
For there among the mounds of fate,
  I read her name upon a stone.

LOVE IS BUT A SLENDER TETHER.

To my love I've sent my greeting,
And though far apart to-day,
    We will have another meeting,
For my letter's on its way.

Out it flies, with swiftest motion,
From the city o'er the land ; —
    On it speeds with true devotion
Till it finds the waiting hand.

Now the seal I see her breaking,
And our lips they almost meet ;
    For my heart to her is speaking
From the dainty little sheet.

Thus again we are together,
And our lives this truth imparts ; —
    Love is but a slender tether
Holding firm the strongest hearts.

TO ONLY SEE WHAT NOW I DREAM.

I OFTEN dream of boyhood times,
Of scenes that now have passed away ;
  They fill my mind with more than rhymes
And turn my gloominess away.

I live once more in days gone by,
Each youthful scene repeats the strain ;
  These spells with me will only die
When memory shall break the chain.

I'd like to stroll down by the shore,
And hear again the murmuring tide ; —
  Where I but dreamed, and nothing more,
Where genial spirits coincide.

I'd like to see my old school books,
That now have passed to other hands ;
  I'd like to read their notes and looks
More distant now than distant lands.

I'd like to see that mother's face,
That gave my boyhood tide its gleam ;
  I'd pay the toll and fall from grace,
To only see what now I dream.

AT NEWPORT CLIFFS.

I STOOD at night upon the cliffs
   That sternly face the Newport sea ; —
And watched the breakers rolling in,
   And heard their wild, sad minstrelsy.

The moon was in its splendor bright,
   Its pale light falling on the sea,
That leaped and pranced among the crags
   That moved to sway in melody.

Above my head the palace soared,
   Below me stood the fisher's cot ;
I saw the scene that favored both
   And felt the wisdom that it taught.

A TALE OF LOVE.

In the sunset's golden splendor,
I beheld a tale of love ;
    And it came with visions tender,
From the scene I saw above.

In the meadow I was lying,
With the river close in view ; —
    While the sun in grandeur dying,
Made its ever fond adieu.

For there like a lover parting,
Stood the sun with ling'ring glance :
    While the river still departing,
Swept along in vigilance.

Like a maiden seemed the evening,
Kissed by sunset's fond adieu ;
    And the morn in brighter meaning
Spoke the lover firm and true.

THE ESCAPE.

Dying in a prison ward
  A wounded convict lay ;
His head pillowed by a pard
  Who wore the prison gray.

Just at his side a letter,
  Begrimed by frequent care,
And in his cell the jailer
  Sat, in the only chair.

A little pet canary,
  Though doubly caged by fate,
Was singing sweet and cheery
  Within the walls so great.

I am dying, he would say,
  To shield another's wrong ;
Wondering he passed the day,
  At night his soul was gone.

And before he breathed his last
    He rose up in his bed ;—
With his eyes a setting fast,
    In broken accents said :

" I 'm dying, ' Pard ! ' —I'm dying !
    I 've scaled the wall this time ;
I hear the guards, they 're firing
    Along the watchful line !

"Say ' Pard ! ' they 'll be suspended !
    They're shooting wide to-night ; "—
And here his soul ascended
    From darkness into light !

THE PUBLIC GIVER.

I 'm a great public giver,
  On the European plan,
That is, the receiver
  Must say I am the man !

Now, in a great city,   .
  To the cream of the town,
If I'm a fair reader,
  He gave a million down !

For the handsomest college
  That the money could build,
For the good of all knowledge
  To the very well filled !

But not for the poor and studious,
  Who are without the means,
But for the rich and luxurious
  Who wallow in gleams.

For the poor can never enter
   That great bronzen door !
It is only for the scholar
   With his volumes of lore.

And the name of the giver
   Will be chiseled in stone !
As a fitting reminder
   And for the deed atone.

The poor are still hungry !
   The sick are in bed !
But heed not the needy
   And feed the well fed !

And in your donation
   If you'd make a big spread,
A college is the notion
   For it *stands* when you 're *dead*.

THE BRIDE OF A YEAR.

ASLEEP near the tomb, mid flowers in bloom,
The bride of a year now peacefully rests ;
　In her wedding gown, they have laid her down,
While a true woman's worth more fully it tests.

　Asleep in its crib, in snowy white bib,
A babe with many a ringlet of gold ;
　Tells plainly the rest, and proof of the test,
That a true woman's worth can never be told.

　A life here on earth and a life at birth,
The bride of a year in a moment has given ;
　But a mother at heart knows only her part,
And the truth of her love leads the way into heaven.

　And now while it sleeps, or cunningly creeps,
This babe, which many a sorrow has wrought,

Tells the bride of a year found motherhood dear,
While a true woman's heart can never be bought.

And there by the tomb, mid flowers in bloom,
Though the bride of a year be a saint now in heaven :
Stands this lesson of love, that came from above,
When our Saviour for sinners was given.

TO A TEA POT.

Dull urn, like harper of the self-same tune
That promotes a charm to the old maid's doom !
Methinks the abler bards have failed to sing
Of such as thee, meek inferior thing ; —
And yet, neglecting thee within their verse
But proves thy gain was with the reverse.
For left to the elderly virgin's tongue
Thou hast, throughout the world already sung,
With note more pleasing to the general ear
Than sweeter strains, no matter how they veer.
For who has not mused o'er the steaming pot,
While sweeter strains remain unsought ?
Yes, many a poet has sung and gone,
While thy dull unmetered hum goes on !
Old maids ! beware ! I warn attend the urn,
For poets soon may have their sumptuous turn
And vie with far more sweeter strains
Than thy simple, hissing urn maintains.

THE DYING GULL.

OFT hast thou soared in dizzy flight
But now thy course deludes thy sight ; —
And boldly plunged into the main
That chills thy heart, that yields the pain.
Poor bird ! kind death hath hushed thine ear
To those who know thou art so dear ; —
Who from the cliff, that fronts the sea,
Call, call in vain, in vain for thee !
And now thy mate moves o'er thy head
To turn in swiftness from the dead ; —
For death's last sleep hath closed thine eye,
And the great waves that pass thee by
Murmur a sad dirge on the way,
For a spirit hath flown away.

THE CURSE OF THE DAY.

'T is the curse of the day, I sing in my lay
  This great disregard for the poor of our clan —
Where gold in our sight, makes greater our right
  And the owner by far a much better man.

'T is the curse of the day, in this land of fair play,
  Where the almighty dollar makes justice a bear —
And criminals are gay, through their own moneyed
      sway,
  While of vapor our laws have more than a share.

'T is the curse of the day, let it be where it may
  When poor little children are slaved for our gain,
'T is a curse and a sin that our greed takes to win
  When money with us has so potent an aim.

'T is the curse of the day, I think you will say,
  This merely "don't care" for the lives we destroy ;

And linemen may roast, at the top of each post
   When a company's money can others employ.

'T is the curse of the day, now think as you may,
   When our fast gaining wealth is held by the few —
And our saints must discern, while ministers learn
   That the Kingdom of Heaven is lost to our view.

ARE WE PULLING OTHERS DOWN?

In this world of fleeting chances,
　　Where we all desire renown,
Do we thrive by mean advances,
　　Are we pulling others down?

Did you gain your place by merit,
　　Have you worked on honest ground ; —
Unassuming is the ferret,
　　Are you pulling others down?

Are you sure you were elected,
　　Do you own the envied crown ; —
Have you craft and fraud rejected,
　　Are you pulling others down?

Did you win your love by fairness,
　　Was your suit with truth profound ; —
Have you left no heart in sadness,
　　Are you pulling others down?

In this world so great with pleasure,
  Are you spreading cares around ; —
Have you crushed some struggling creature:
  Are you pulling others down ?

Have you felt the pangs of hunger,
  Do you look for true renown ?
Rise by helping one another,
  Love can never pull you down.

Lift the fallen, soothe the wretched !
  Let your life with good abound ; —
All are great with this respected,
  None shall rise by pulling down !

THE SONG OF THE RIVULET.

SILENTLY stealing through the field,
Gliding away, slipping away,
  Winding along, singing its song
Of the meadow and the field.

Sweeping through the shady grove,
Wider the brook, trouty the nook —
  Surging along, singing its song
Of the woodland and the grove.

Dashing widely over the ledge
Breaking its thrall, leaping the fall,
  Splashing along, singing its song
Of the highland and the ledge.

Swiftly sweeping over the moor,
Deeper the glide, nearer the tide,

Gurgling along, singing its song
Of the marshland and the moor.

Leaping at last into the sea,
Now hear its roar, along the shore,
Rolling along, singing its song
Of the ocean and the sea.

THEODORE BEANE.

THERE 's a footprint for the purest snow,
  A death-knock for the slighted door ;—
There's a rough impression of sorrow
  That each heart alone must endure.

Each hearthstone has its dying ember,
  That lingers on with feeble glow :—
Each fireside has its elder member
  That while others stay it must go.

And thus 't is those that dying leave us,
  That light the pathway to the goal,
That otherwise would seem most grievous,
  To the weary wandering soul !

For death, like the snow that's falling,
  On this cheerless wint'ry day,
Is with its mission calling
  Hopeful Spring on her joyous way.

BARON MONOPOLY.

I'M Baron Monopoly
A monarch more properly,
And curse to the wage-working band ;
My aim is monopoly
I want the more properly
The wealth, of this broad yielding land.

I'm Baron Monopoly
A ruler more properly,
And serf to the gold-brooding clan :
My thirst is monopoly
Or heart the more properly
Is not with the down-trodden man.

I'm Baron Monopoly
A king the more properly
And despot as others have been ;
But force of monopoly
Is guard to me properly
And check to all ignorant men.

But Baron Monopoly
When people more properly,
Shall have seen the little they ken ;
Thy head will be properly
A barren monopoly
As many a tyrant's has been.

STILL THE RIVER GLIDES AWAY.

Autumn days are fast advancing,
  Fields and meadows now are brown,
Gayer hues are yet enhancing
  Fairest Autumn's golden crown.

Still the river keeps its pleasure,
  Spreading leaves and blossoms wide,
While the Summer's fullest measure
  Yields to Autumn's coming tide.

Aye! the river runs forever
  Mirroring now the Autumn day,
And though seasons thus may sever
  Still the river glides away.

DR. G. FELIX MATTHES.

OLD friend ! thou tried and trusted one,
  In youthful days I knew thee well ;—
Familiar face when ills begun,
  To thee I tend the last farewell !

Though many pains thou hast deceived,
  The Great Physician knew thy cure ;
And though by death alone relieved,
  Thy skillful worth will long endure.

Fulfillment this, thy final " call,"
  " Prescription " we in time receive ; —
With restoration for us all
  Who this Physician do believe.

The humble mound ! the peaceful home !
  Will give her tired children rest ;—

This mound is thine ! this heart thine own,
  A home for all is surely blest.

And far beyond this restful spot
  Where care and misery lose their way ; —
I hear this truth by spirits wrought,
  "The Doctor 's in," they seem to say.

THY SONG'S ITS OWN AND GOD WITHIN.

SING, little birds upon the branches,
Merry warblers of the Spring ;
　Pleasing to me the varied fancies
Thou art yearly wont to bring.

　Refreshing now thy Spring-time ditty
Above the city's noisy din :
　Though lost to many, what's the pity,
Thy song 's its own and God within.

　Perplexed with life that seems so dreary,
I yearn for thy freedom more :
　And that from which I 'd never weary
Is the least of all thy store.

ONLY A BRAKEMAN.

THESE are the words we hear every day
  As we pass the crossing gate,
"Only a brakeman" over the way,
  Killed by the down-coming freight.

Only a brakeman, that is all !
  Lying dead on the coal-house floor ;—
In answer to the whistle's call
  A member of the down brakes corps !

Only a coroner, that is all !
  Attending now the final rites ;—
"Only a brakeman," that is all !
  That he in his diary writes.

Only a home, forever gone !
  Only a face, forever sad !
This is the railroad's daily song
  As they wave their blood-colored flag.

Only a company, getting rich !
 In an undertaker's style,
With a life for every switch
 And a funeral for every mile !

Only a God, that is all !
 President in a better clime —
Where none smash up, nor brakemen fall,
 And they make their regular time.

A LIKELIHOOD.

THE river runs beneath my feet,
  The waters sparkle in the sun :—
With me my days are quite as fleet
  As on the stream of time they run.

A humble birth, the merest start,
  And soon I reached the river's side ;—
A little light the darker part
  And now among the surges glide.

And through the bridge I'll whirl at last
  Quite worn with froth and foam of time ;
For in the waters sweeping past
  I see a fate resembling mine.

ODE TO A MOSQUITO.

—

Vain minstrel of the evening train
There is no charm within thy strain :
And why persistent wilt thou play
To me, who cares not for thy lay ?

Away ! disturber of my sleep !
And force me not my vow to keep,
Nor stay to tune thy airy harp,
As though thou play'st with any sharp.

Dull bird ! thy simple, touching strain
Imparts more truth than I proclaim ;—
For I have heard that from thy note
The very best musicians quote !
That music grave or gay depends
Upon the sounds that nature lends.

How now ! for this audacious bird
Can I forgive the cheek bestirred,

If notes that charm this ear of mine
But signify what *has* been thine?

And yet I ne'er can wear the ore,
Though the diamond be its core : —
So I reject thy serenade,
Although it has a Mozart made.

DYING ALONE.

PASSING away !
Within the gloom of squalid home,
A worn and wearied woman lay ; —
Waiting for death, waiting alone !

Dying alone !
Without one little word of cheer : —
With feet alike the coldest stone –
And now another night is near.

Dying for bread !
Within the sound of Christian ears ; —
Without a hand to hold her head
Or wipe away her choking tears.

Dying at last !
While lingers now one feeble spark ; —
A little quiver, all is past !
Her soul has left the room so dark.

Now stiff and cold !
Within the shade of churchy gray ; —
And *none* will close her lips and fold
Those arms of weary working clay.

Rotten and foul !
The nose of human aid is keen ; —
And but for this and tenant's growl,
She'd been there *now*, for all I've seen !

But found at last !
She's borne like beast to hiding grave ! --
Her lonely death repeats the past
That man neglects, but God will save !

A CHARACTERISTIC.

I MET a dog the other day
    Upon a corner crossing,
Who bore the marks of bloody fray
    And quite a recent tossing.

The cuts were thick upon his back,
    One eye was closed completely,
And leaving gore with every track,
    Along he moved obliquely.

A tear-drop lurked within the eye
    With which he navigated ;
And though run down by passer-by.
    Not he who execrated.

Now, when a man is thus undone
    And likewise gets a licking,

The ear he wants of every one
  And chance to do his kicking.

And though the dog I met this day
  Would halt and gaze astounded,
To none had he a word to say,
  Indeed he was dumbfounded.

THE BROKEN VASE.

BESIDE you humbly mounded grave,
    Wherein some form now lowly lies,
A broken vase imparts the love,
    That a withered flower implies !

The sweetness of its dying blush
    Has sought a milder atmosphere,
And like the soul that leaves the dust,
    To move within another sphere.

The grave is but the broken vase
    Wherein we place the treasured gem,
To meet with that mysterious fate
    That claims a wisdom over men !

Lone inmate of this shaded spot,
    The solitude of death is thine !
I, too, some day will share thy lot
    And but await unfolding time.

The churchyard gloom shall then be mine,
  O ! will some stranger gently place
A fragrant blooming jessamine
  Within *my* stained and broken vase !

That it may stop some passer-by
  To look upon its wilted sedge,
And think, as I have learned to sigh,
  The fragrance of its life is fled.

I SAUNTER BY THE COMING TIDE.

I SAUNTER by the coming tide,
  Alone upon the sea-strewn shore,
And yet forever at my side
  There seems a spirit wand'ring o'er.

The cold, dull rumbling of the sea
  Beguiles me with that sweeter lay
That touched our souls in harmony
  And moved our hearts but in one way.

I linger by the well-known seat
  Where oft I named the stars above,
And there, again, thy fond retreat
  But moves me to thee in my love.

O' soul ! art thou forever gone,
  Or dost thou sometimes seem with me?
And do I sit but here alone
  Or am I on the shore with thee?

EIN ZWEITER HANS SACHS.

(*Staats Zeitung*, Portland, Oregon.)

THE late Julius Kirschbaum, shoemaker, who died at
New Bedford, March 27th, 1893, left unpublished works to
the amount of nineteen plays, twenty-three manuscripts
of miscellaneous writings, and eighteen manuscripts of
poems.—*New Bedford Standard.*

THE shop is closed ! the cobbler 's dead !
Of shoes to mend he 'd had his share ; —
   The weary days ! the cares of lead !
Have vanished all into the air.

   It was no bell of six o'clock
That bade this humble man be done ; —
   Though thrown aside the cobbler's frock,
His daily work had scarce begun.

   The book is closed ! the pen is still !
The midnight lamp shall burn no more ; —
   If every heart but had my fill
Thy praise would ring from shore to shore.

Rest, cobbler, poet ; time will tell
The nobler work thy pen has wrought ; —
   The many shoes you've cobbled well,
The bitter battle you have fought !

   The cobbler 's dead ! a poet reigns !
His home shall be the hearts of men ; —
   Who would have thought he had the brains,
This humble man, a man of men ?

I WANDERED WITH THE MUSE APACE.

I WANDERED with the muse apace,
Where surging billows seek the shore ---
 I gazed upon their easy grace,
And felt this common truth the more.

How little here is potent man,
When moved by one reflective thought --
 The merest pebble we may scan
That smaller now the waves have wrought.

The sail-white speck that fades away,
The glimmer of the beacon light ; ---
 A mere reflection on the bay,
In God's own greatness but a slight.

THE MILL ON THE DAMN-SIDE.

A CORPORATION skirts the town,
   Polluting every germ of health
By hiring children scarcely grown,
   While they speed on toward wealth.

The mill suggests ! the curse survives !
   Of slaving children for their gain ;
While social law protects their lives
   And boldly will their rights sustain.

The notice hangs within their doors,
   But only for the blind to read,
For this is what they tell their boys,
   If they to sixty hours agreed.

A lock is on this prison door,
   A watch is stationed at the gate ;
They care not for the ten-hour law
   And spurn the orders of our State !

They 'd hire our babes when first they creep,
 If they could spin the twisted thread ; —
They figure *only* what is cheap
 And know the need is daily bread !

Our town is small, but wide awake
 To an illegal glass of beer ; —
And well offenders know their fate
 When they attempt the traffic here.

The mill still here polluting thrives,
 Defiant to all posted laws !
And children more will slave their lives
 Before they 'll fear the eagle's claws !

The mill still rules ! the curse survives !
 'T is twisted in their very thread,
'T will spool upon their moneyed lives
 And follow them when they are dead !

FOR A SOLDIER IS IN THE ROOM.

—

Alone in thought and meditation,
Brooding o'er the wasted past ; —
    Finding no alleviation
And fearful of the coming blast ; —
    Haunted by a reproachful vision,
Knowing the morrow grants no change.
    Longing for the peaceful mission
And departure from life's dark range.

And I gaze upon the picture
That hangs suspended from the wall ; —
    Soldier-like in every feature
Prolific of his sad downfall.
    With a look of deep emotion
Alone in his rock-bound seat ; —
    Looking far out on the ocean
A "Waterloo" beyond retreat !

And my hopes are growing brighter
For a soldier is in the room —

And my cares now seem the lighter
In the great Napoleon's gloom !
    And who, in meditation,
No matter how bowed down with care,
    Cannot find alleviation
In another's far greater share ?

A MEMORIAL TRIBUTE.

SAGE, I a poor and studious recluse,
  Do here invoke the presence of the muse,
And vie to thee my humbly metered strain,
  The least of all in thy memorial train ; —
Should insignificance share with my verse,
  My skill but fails to cope my heart's reverse ;
But should, though indistinct, some kindly word
  Scarce mention what thou hast already heard,
Perceive that I have thanked the *Whittier*
  For what the world hath called the seer ;
And though thy harp is stayed by weaker grasp,
  Thy songs now teach the art is not in clasp ;
But that it is of pure celestial fire,
  That fills thy heart and vibrates from thy lyre.
Sing on ! O, bard ! in thy melodious way,
  To be original is thine every lay.

OTHER DAYS.

I STAND again upon the shore
   Where rumbling falls the heaving bay ; —
And since I've heard these waters roar
   A swift decade has passed away.

A swift decade of flying years
   Has swept across this restless deep,
Since I along these rocky piers
   Have seen the gathering billows sweep.

Again, the sound of gurgling tide
   My willing thoughts with rapture fill ; —
And as the breakers near me glide
   I feel the same familiar thrill.

'T was here when hard oppressed I 'd stroll
   And leave my load upon the way ; —
For here beside the breakers' roll
   My cares seemed like the foaming spray.

And oft along the foam-flecked strand
 I've met some little ones at play ; —
And writing names upon the sand
 They'd laugh at mine they couldn't say !

And from yon high and craggy cliff
 I've watched the ships file out to sea ; —
And seen the breezes freshening stiff,
 Full speed them on in company.

But now, alone, unknown I stand,
 My crowding thoughts I cannot keep ; —
For time and years, their days have spread,
 As ships upon the widening deep.

LIFE.

Just a highway leading upward
And a tramp of many miles ; —
   All of us are pressing onward,
Some in pains and some in smiles.

Hot and dusty is the highway,
Cooling shades are sought in vain ; —
   Time and thrift usurp the by-way,
We who win must work to gain.

Night affords her restful pleasure,
Morn reveals our needs again ; —
   And the tramp's incessant measure
We must still take up again.

Till infirm our step and weary
With the journey yet undone,
   All around is dark and dreary —
Life begins ! the journey 's done !

A POET'S FANCY TAKES ME.

A POET's fancy takes me
Down by the silvery stream ;
　A poet's dream awaits me
Where mirroring waters gleam.

A spirit face will greet me
Down by the wayward stream ;
　A magic spell now leads me
Where only poets dream.

A poet's song shall thrill me,
Unuttered though it be ;
　A poet's love shall fill me,
Though song may never be !

WHEN SOME MEN DIE.

THE bells will toll for the brave and the true,
And our saddened hearts wear a sombre hue ; —
    The stores will be closed and flags at half-mast,
For this is our way, and long may it last, —
        When some men die !

Our flow'ry mounds in profusion relate
The peace we wish to the body in state :—
    And the quiet mien of sexton we see,
Brings to our minds he will yet come for thee, –
        When some men die !

The funerals will pass with pomp and show,
And the turning wheels will tell where they go ;—
    To mix with the earth and of nature take
The very same share that none of us shake, —
        When some men die !

While a pauper's grave we will often find,
Yet those ne'er missed leave no trouble behind ; –

And quick to their rest without pomp or show,
The old sexton's cart could tell where they go,—
   When some men die!

The wealthy provide for their next of kin,
Though it oft proves a stake that lawyers win ; —
   Of course they will make some public bequest,
If it was n't for this they never could rest, —
   When some men die !

And when men are gone, if we only knew,
Or if half we hear should ever prove true,—
   The eye of the needle 's the largest of holes,
Or some of them have the smallest of souls,—
   When some men die !

CHIMES SWEET WITH MUSIC TO MY EAR.

I SIT by my window and listen
　　To the sweetly chiming bells ;
And their melody seems to christen
　　My soul with wondrous spells.

And I gaze upon the moonlight,
　　As it fills the street below ; —
Mirroring happy faces bright,
　　And many full sad with woe.

For now, I see a pleading vagrant,
　　Who vainly asks for bread —
As she totters along the pavement
　　Wishing ! wishing ! to be dead !

Chimes, sweet with music to my ear,
　　Move her to better things below ; --
Teach as well the mighty million
　　Good and better deeds to show.

THE POET'S FATE.

The moon beams forth in grandeur,
    Piercing the darkening gloom ; —
The night is bathed in splendor,
    And bright is the poet's room.

The world 's abed and sleeping
    And the midnight guard moves on ; —
While he his vigil keeping,
    With the old rejected song !

And poets live and vanish
    Like the shadows of a night ; —
They sing, and starve, and languish,
    While the world is ever bright.

An attic and a rag-heap
    Tells where they sung and died ; —

And Muses paid their visits
  Where cities point with pride !

And this is true salvation,
  And still the ready fate ; —
For Muses court starvation
  While fools grow fat with state.

MY MOTHER'S GRAVE.

I STOOD beside the place to-day
 And looked upon the grass-grown mound,
Wherein my dear, good mother lay,
 At rest in death, asleep profound !

 I lingered long beside the spot,
  The essential grave, the chiseled stone ; -
With heavy heart in sadness fraught
  I left, as I had come, alone !

 But with each step there seemed to come
  A spirit quite along the street ; -
That brought to mind my dear old home,
  Now gone ! forever obsolete !

 I tried my mind to occupy,
  With fancies of a different mood ; --
But the spirit seemed forever by,
  Hasten or linger as I would.

I leaned against the old stone wall
  And brushed the tell-tale tears away,
Filled with a mother's fervent call,
  Her treasured precepts to obey !

And the haunt then seemed to leave me,
  As I journeyed my away along ; —
Other thoughts came up before me
  And gave the finish to my song.

SHIPS THAT NEVER SAIL

In my hours of needed leisure,
    Sad with life's tumultuous sway,
Ethereal tends my pleasure
    Though my fetters bid me stay !

Thoughts alike are coming, going,
    Building ships that never sail !
Coursing rivers never flowing,
    Making time an idle tale !

Though vain are all my fancies,
    Scarcely uttered into thought ; —
Were the painter's treasured pansies
    Just the soulless things he wrought ?

Softly, then, with your reflection,
    On this poorly metered rhyme ;

'T is a chord of my affection
Slowly coming into time !

God may make and rule the ocean,
Man, the ships that *he* can scale ; —
But forever my creation
Be the ships that never sail.

WELCOME.

There 's a motto famed for meaning
In the room just o'er the way,
  And from worsted work I'm gleaning
What to others I will say.

Welcome, is the word that 's woven,
In the frame just o'er the door,
  And could needle-work have spoken
'T would have said it o'er and o'er.

The little nymph now sleeping
On the bed so clean and white,
  Is the wisdom and in keeping
Of the motto I would write.

My kisses with her slumber,
On those lips so sweetly meek,
  And I 'll never tell the number
I have placed upon her cheek.

From her baby face I 'm gleaning
In the twilight of her sleep —
  Just the symbol and the meaning
Of the motto all should keep.

  For she came in days of sadness, —
I had long been out of work, —
  And she filled our home with gladness
With her cunning little chirp.

  And she pays with love's caresses —
'T was by this our hearts she won ; —
  She has mamma's golden tresses,
She 's our little '' welcome '' one !

THESE WORDS ARE BUT ITS KNELL.

I SOUGHT the quiet woods to-day,
And roamed about the pine-tree grove,—
    Where peace and nature led the way
And fancy's thoughts were free to rove.

I watched the day's declining light
Steal softly silent from my view ;—
    And felt the cool and quiet night
Had bid my worldly cares adieu.

O ! thou calm and rapturous spot !
Had men and minds thy peaceful lore —
    How sweet and lasting then their lot
And scarce the damning hue of more.

While far removed from busy care,
At distant sound of vesper bell
    I felt this touch of earnest prayer,
And know these words are but its knell !

PEG! PEG! PEG!

Peg! Peg! peg!
All day in thy cobbler's shop ; —
Peg! Peg! Peg!
Some day thy labor will stop.

Peg! Peg! Peg!
Thou must send thy boys to school ; —
Peg! Peg! Peg!
But stick to thy lowly stool.

Peg! Peg! Peg!
With heart both cheery and gay : —
Peg! Peg! Peg!
Is now the tune of thy lay.

Peg! Peg! Peg!
As the hours roll swiftly past ; —
Peg! Peg! Peg!
But think of the gifts thou hast.

Sing ! Sing ! Sing !
All day in thy cobbler's shop ; —
Sing ! Sing ! Sing !
Some day thy hammer will stop.

Sing ! Sing ! Sing !
With heart both cheery and gay ; –
Sing ! Sing ! Sing !
The songs for thy brighter day.

Sing ! Sing ! Sing !
All day in thy humble sphere ; —
Sing ! Sing ! Sing !
The morn of thy night is near.

Sing ! Sing ! Sing !
All day on thy lowly stool ; —
Sing ! Sing ! Sing !
The truth of thy life shall rule.

TIME 'S A MIRROR HELD BEFORE THEE.

I STOOD by the roadside dreaming
  Of the great men who had gone;
And the scene gave out the seeming,—
  Still the world is moving on.

Aye, the day foretells the morrow,
  As the hours roll on their way;
Nature halts not in our sorrow,
  All with time shall pass away.

And though men of rank may leave us,
  Still the world will run the same;—
Towns will grow and cities prosper,
  'T is in common—such is fame.

Men of greatness mark the future
  Of our ever present day,

And all our lives are miniature
  In the world's progressive sway.

            *

Time 's a mirror held before thee,
  That reflects thy presence here ; —
A moment, and the glass without thee
  Still reveals the whirling sphere.

DISCONTENTMENT IS THE STORY.

ETERNAL nature leads the way,
    My circling path is through the wood,
Where scarce the sunbeams cast a ray,
    And heat of day is there withstood.

Lost to the gazing world and throng,
    I while a time in haunts like these,
Nor sigh for what the most may long
    A mind content and well at ease.

Beyond me lies the hill-side town
    At rest in its summer glory,
And there men fret in their renown --
    Discontentment is the story !

THE OLD MILL AT NANTUCKET.

A SONG I sing of old Nantucket —
   For many years I've been the mill —
Full every one has kicked the bucket
   Whom first I saw upon the hill.

I've seen the town both young and old,
   I know this lonely island's past,
I've stood it well, so I am told,
   And many years have yet to last.

Of noble deeds I've seen a score ;
   Of shipwrecked sailors brave and true ;
I've heard the ocean's wildest roar
   And seen its waters calm and blue.

I've seen the jail close on its prey,
   I've heard the ablest lawyer's plea ;
I've seen our sainted ones full gay,
   And hardest sinners bend the knee.

I've seen our ships go down to sea
   And sailors make their last adieu ;
I've seen the worst of foes agree
   And lovers' vows stand firm and true.

I've seen the town vote no and yes,
   I've watched the tippler to his grave ;
I've seen it sold where none could guess,
   And never yet have been its slave.

I've seen the building of hotels,
   And know the kick of Summer bills ;
I've heard the talk of city belles,
   And quite prefer my lonely ills.

For on these guests I yearly thrive,
   And though my shingles slip away,
I stand the test and keep alive,
   And with their nickels make it pay.

MY SONG HAS TAKEN FLIGHT.

At my window now I'm dreaming,
  In the calm of evening time,
While the stars above are teeming
  With their melody of rhyme.

Dazed with dreams too bright for paper,
  Wrapped in songs too sweet to hear ; —
Wonder not they 're lost in vapor,
  Ere I come to place them here.

Though I yield with true submission,
  And my mind is free to write,
Still to echo turns my mission,
  For my song has taken flight.